W9-ARZ-765

The Spotlight Club Mysteries

●

THE MYSTERY OF THE SILVER TAG
THE MYSTERY OF THE MISSING SUITCASE
THE HIDDEN BOX MYSTERY
MYSTERY AT MACADOO ZOO
THE MYSTERY OF THE WHISPERING VOICE
MYSTERY OF THE MELTING SNOWMAN
MYSTERY OF THE BEWITCHED BOOKMOBILE
MYSTERY OF THE VANISHING VISITOR
MYSTERY OF THE LONELY LANTERN
MYSTERY AT KEYHOLE CARNIVAL
MYSTERY OF THE MIDNIGHT MESSAGE
MYSTERY AT SOUTHPORT CINEMA
MYSTERY OF THE MUMMY'S MASK

A Spotlight Club Mystery

Mystery of the Mummy's Mask

Florence Parry Heide and Roxanne Heide

Illustrations by Seymour Fleishman

ALBERT WHITMAN & COMPANY, Chicago

Library of Congress Cataloging in Publication Data

Heide, Florence Parry.
Mystery of the Mummy's Mask.

(Pilot books)
SUMMARY: The discovery of an ancient mummy's mask involves the Spotlight Club detectives with unscrupulous art dealers and danger.
[1. Mystery and detective stories] I. Heide, Roxanne, joint author. II. Fleishman, Seymour. III. Title.
PZ7.H36Myi [Fic] 78-31728
ISBN 0-8075-5384-0

Published simultaneously in Canada by
General Publishing, Limited, Toronto.

Contents

1 • *The Newspaper Business*

"WHY ARE RIVERS RICH?" Jay Temple asked. He was sitting at the kitchen table, surrounded by papers.

Cindy Temple looked at her brother and sighed. "I've heard that one before."

"I haven't," said their next-door neighbor and best friend, Dexter Tate. "Why are rivers rich?"

"Because they all have two banks," Jay said. He leaned back and roared with laughter.

Cindy rolled her eyes at Dexter. "Nobody home upstairs, I'm afraid," she said, tapping her pencil against her head.

"If you're going to be in charge of the riddles

and jokes for our newspaper, you have to come up with better jokes than that," Dexter said.

"Okay, okay," Jay said sheepishly. "I know the *Random Review* deserves better."

Cindy turned to Dexter. "Did you get anyone else to place an ad in our paper?"

Dexter nodded. "Yesterday. The Donut Hole liked the last three issues of the *Random Review* so much that they signed up again," he said proudly. "And I signed up Southport Cinema, too. And World Wide Arts." He paused. "That's the good news."

Jay looked at Dexter. "What's up? Is there bad news, too?"

"Looks like it," Dexter admitted. "When I was riding my bike back from World Wide Arts yesterday I came down Corrigan Way. Past Mr. Pruitt's house."

"He's the best customer we have in our lawn-mowing business," Jay said.

"Not any more, I'm afraid," Dexter said gloomily.

"Why?" Jay asked. "What did he tell you?"

"Nothing. I didn't talk to him. I saw him

standing in his front window, but he sort of ducked out of the way as if he didn't want me to see him. There was a truck parked in front of his house. The sign on the truck said 'Lon's Lawn Service.' And there was a big guy in an orange shirt doing our job."

Jay looked puzzled. "That's strange. Mr. Pruitt liked us, I know he did. And he liked our work. I guess we lost out to a bigger company."

"Isn't Mr. Pruitt the one who works with the Gilliland Museum here in Kenoska?" Cindy asked.

Dexter and Jay nodded.

"Well," Cindy said cheerfully, "you may have lost one customer, but that doesn't mean you can't find others."

"I guess you're right," Jay grumbled. He tapped his pencil and looked at Dexter. "Give me those names again for the ads."

Dexter repeated the information and Jay jotted the names down in a column in his notebook. He scribbled a few figures and brightened. "Hey, guess what? We just need one more store to place an ad in the paper for this issue. Then we'll have enough money to cover the cost of the printing."

"If we keep this up, we'll be the most successful newspaper in Kenoska," Dexter said. "Who knows? Maybe we'll all end up being reporters."

"In addition to being detectives," Cindy reminded him.

Dexter snapped his fingers. "We could put an ad in for ourselves—a Spotlight Club ad."

Cindy laughed. "Why not? It could read like this: 'Have a mystery? Detectives Jay and Cindy Temple and Dexter Tate at your service. We've solved other mysteries, and we can solve yours.' "

"Makes us sound pretty professional," Jay said. "And why not? We are."

Cindy looked at the piles of paper jumbled on the kitchen table. "It's lucky we have the rest of the day to get the copy for the *Random Review* finished. The printer doesn't need it until five, and we'll need all that time."

"Lucky for us Mom's been willing to type up everything," Jay said. "Even if she says her fingers are frazzled."

Dexter looked at the paste-up that Cindy was working on. It was a sheet of 8½-by-11-inch paper divided into two columns. Cindy was neatly pasting down typed stories in each column. At the top of the page big letters said "Random Review." When the paste-up was finished, Dexter was going to take it to the printer.

"What about your column 'Susie's Super Advice'?" Dexter asked. "Did anyone write to you?"

Cindy nodded. She shuffled through a pile of letters and read: " 'Dear Susie: A new boy moved in across the street last month. He's cute, but he hasn't noticed me yet. What can I do? Signed, Frustrated in Kenoska.' "

"What's your answer going to be?" asked Jay.

"Make lots of noise," Cindy told him.

Dexter glanced at the kitchen clock. "If I've got to find one more person to buy an ad for our paper, I'd better hurry." He stood up and stretched. "Lucky my bike and I are in such great shape."

"Are you still trying to win that T-shirt by riding your bike a million miles this summer?" asked Jay.

Dexter nodded. "Not a million, exactly, just a measly three hundred. I combine bike riding with my job of advertising salesman for the *Random Review.*"

"How many miles have you pedaled so far?" asked Cindy.

"I don't know. I don't want to add up all the miles until the first week is over. I just keep a chart of the miles I do every day. That way I'll be surprised when I add them all together."

Dexter pushed his glasses up on his nose and started out the door. "I'm off to find one more ad for today's issue," he said.

"Okay," said Cindy. "Remember, we've got to get the ad pasted up before five."

"I know," said Dexter, letting the door slam.

He got his bike and headed down the country road just outside town. He remembered seeing some small stores along that road. Maybe one of the owners would be interested in placing an ad in the *Random Review*.

It had really been a great idea of Cindy's to start a neighborhood newspaper, Dexter thought. This would be the fourth issue, and already people were commenting on what a good job the three Spotlighters had done.

And publishing a newspaper wasn't too hard. Cindy had found a book about it at the library. The book showed how to type the news in columns, how to make headlines, and how to paste everything up neatly, ready to be printed.

Dexter's job was to get enough people to buy advertising space so there would be money to pay for the paper and the printing. Jay helped with the paste-up, kept track of the money, and made sure the copy got to the printer on time. Cindy was in charge of the news and the advice column. The Spotlighters were a pretty good team, and they put out a pretty good newspaper.

The first store Dexter came to had a big sign hanging on the door: "Closed for vacation."

Dexter sighed and kept going. He hoped the next store wouldn't be closed, too. He glanced at his odometer and raised his eyebrows. He had already pedaled six miles! It didn't seem as if he had come that far. In no time he would have ridden enough miles to get the T-shirt. He would add all his daily miles up on Saturday, but not until then. He liked setting the odometer back to zero to see how far he rode each day.

When Dexter came to Abe's Market, he was relieved to find that it was open. He parked his bike and walked inside. A little bell jingled as the door swung shut behind him. He walked over to a scratched counter where a couple of last week's copies of the *Random Review* were stacked.

A small, round woman stood behind the counter, with her back to him, trying to stock some shelves above her head.

"These shelves get taller every year," she muttered.

"Here, let me help," Dexter offered.

"Oh!" she gasped. "I didn't hear you, sonny.

Thought I was alone." She let Dexter take the boxes and put them up on a shelf.

"My goodness," the woman wheezed. "Thanks, sonny, thanks much." She shook her head in appreciation. "Didn't know they made 'em like you anymore. These days, people just bust in the door, want their milk right away, no time to waste. Hurry, hurry, hurry." She wiped her hands on a soiled apron tied around her thick waist. "Now, what do you need, sonny?"

Dexter felt embarrassed that he hadn't come to buy anything. He felt in his pocket for change. "I'll just take a box of those raisins," he said.

"Eh?" the woman asked. "Doughnuts, you said?" She shook her head. "No doughnuts here, sonny."

Dexter realized the woman must be almost deaf. "Raisins," he said loudly, pointing to the bright red boxes. The woman smiled, nodded, and reached for one of the boxes. "That's what I thought you said."

Dexter loudly explained about the *Random Review*, showing her last week's issue. When she finally understood, she was happy to pay for an ad.

"You helped me, I'll help you," she said. "I already know your paper." She pointed to the copies on the counter.

Dexter paid for his raisins and left the store, whistling.

Now they had enough money for the printer. He glanced at his watch. It was still early. There was time to pedal a few more miles before he had to turn back. He continued down the country road in the same direction.

By now there were no houses or stores, just fields and ramshackle barns. A few huge shade trees lined the road, and long grass swayed in the breeze. The side roads that branched off were overgrown with weeds. There was very little traffic. It was a peaceful place to ride a bike, Dexter thought.

He recognized an old abandoned house off to the left, quite a distance from the road. He'd passed it many times before. No one had lived there for years, not since Dexter could remember. No one had ever cared enough to repair the house, and now the roof slanted at an odd angle. Dexter decided to ride his bike over and take a closer look.

The driveway that led up to the house was rutted and overgrown with weeds. Dexter watched the ground in front of him, trying to avoid the deep ruts. He was pedaling slowly when he noticed something odd. Fresh tire tracks.

Dexter stopped his bike and got off to examine the tracks. He knew they were fresh because yesterday's heavy rain would have washed old tracks away.

It looked as though someone had driven up this same driveway very recently. Maybe the farmhouse was not deserted, after all.

Strange.

2 • A Deserted Farmhouse?

DEXTER DECIDED to take a look at the farmhouse. Maybe someone had just come to check the house over, to make sure it was okay. Or maybe someone was interested in buying it. There were a dozen possible explanations. After all, Dexter himself was here out of curiosity. And he wasn't the only one in the world with a curious streak!

He walked his bike to the end of the long driveway and parked it near the leaning front porch. Even from where he stood, he could smell the mustiness of the old house.

Dexter liked old houses. He liked to imagine what they must have been like when people lived

in them. A large family could have lived in this house, it was so big.

As Dexter climbed onto the porch, the boards groaned loudly. The steps seemed ready to collapse completely. He shifted his weight carefully and moved toward the door. A battered swing hung from rusted chains, and Dexter gave it a push. The swing screeched, causing him to jump.

He stopped the moving swing and turned to the front door. It had come off one of its hinges and now hung tilted, the wood rotting.

Dexter stepped through the front entrance into a hallway. The musty old-house smell was strong, but he thought he smelled something else, too. Something familiar—but something he couldn't identify. What was it?

The faded wallpaper on the dingy walls was peeling off in layers. Brownish plaster showed where the bottom layer had torn, and in spots where the plaster had worn away, there was still another faded wallpaper of a different pattern.

Dexter walked into what must have been the living room. The wooden floor beneath his feet groaned and squeaked.

It was dim inside. He squinted as he looked around. Old newspapers lay in messy piles on the floor. How many years had they been there? He picked up one and looked at the date. Fifteen years ago. Before he was even born! He put the paper down and wandered into another room.

This must have been the dining room, Dexter decided. A small brass chandelier, tarnished and bent, hung from the ceiling. Dexter imagined a dining table beneath it, a table covered with dishes and food. He could imagine chairs around the table and a family laughing and talking.

Dexter went on to the next room, which seemed even darker than the dining room. There was only one small window, and it was boarded up. He could see an old porcelain sink. This must have been the kitchen. The floor was so slanted Dexter felt for a moment as if he were in a fun house.

Again Dexter smelled that strange smell. It seemed to be in the kitchen, but where? He peered into the sink. Stains made maps all over the surface, but there was something else, too. A pile of ashes?

Dexter bent his head and sniffed. All at once he knew what the odor was. Pipe tobacco. He remembered the smell from his father's pipe. Would tobacco smell that fresh after all these years? Dexter smiled at himself. What was he doing, trying to invent a mystery? He had found fresh tire tracks and now fresh tobacco. So what? Somebody had seen the house and had wanted to look at it, that was all.

Staring into the sink, Dexter suddenly heard a sharp scrabbling noise behind him. He jumped and spun around. Across the room a scrawny cat arched its back, its legs stiff and straight. A low growl escaped the animal's throat before it turned and dashed out of the kitchen.

Dexter let out his breath. This house was beginning to get on his nerves. He looked again around the small kitchen. Something caught his eye on the far side of the counter.

A folded paper. Curious, he picked it up. His eyes widened. The most recent copy of the *Random Review*! What was the Spotlighters' newspaper doing here?

He stared at the *Review,* frowned, and put it back on the counter.

Underneath the paper was a box of doughnuts, half full. Dexter touched one. It was fresh.

A small door off the kitchen led into another room. What had this room been used for? Storage? A den? There was no wallpaper on these walls, just cracked plaster and stains from a leaking roof. Puzzled, Dexter looked at the floor.

Something was different. The floor sloped like

the others, but . . . Dexter snapped his fingers.

No dust, that's what was different. The other floors had been covered with thick dust, but the floor in this room looked recently swept. There weren't any cobwebs like those he'd noticed in the corners of the other rooms. Odd.

Dexter looked around for a broom, but the room was empty. There were no newspapers lying on the floor, nothing. Except . . . what was that? He stared at something near a doorway. It was a thick piece of rope, curled on the floor. One end was under the closed door. Dexter followed the rope, aware that it was new. New like the doughnut box and the *Random Review*.

Dexter wiped his glasses on his sleeve and turned the doorknob. It squeaked loudly. The door opened slowly, as if something held it back. Must be the rope, Dexter thought.

The door finally gave way, and Dexter stood in an even smaller room than the one he had just left. This must have been a storage room or a utility room once, he decided. There was a small window, but the glass was so dirty he could barely see out.

Dexter leaned over to pick up the rope and

struck his head on an overhanging piece of lumber. "Ouch!" he cried, surprised at the loudness of his own voice.

He examined the rope. It was tough and still a fresh yellow color. He rubbed his head and looked around the room. His eyes slowly grew accustomed to the dark, and gradually he could make out something in the corner.

Against the wall was a stack of crates—big boxes with lettering on the sides. There was a ball of rope on the top crate.

Dexter looked at the rope in his hand and back again at the stack of boxes. The same rope, he thought.

One crate stood apart from the others, and Dexter decided to look inside. He wished he could see better. Why didn't the house have more windows? It was a bright, sunny afternoon, but almost no sun came in here.

There was a lid on the crate, and Dexter carefully lifted it. He peered inside. He could see nothing but straw and some pieces of rope. And some of the same ashes he had seen before in the sink. Ashes from pipe tobacco. Someone had been foolish enough to drop ashes in a wooden crate.

Dexter frowned and straightened. An empty room, swept clean. Fresh cord from that room to this one, and then several big crates with some of the same rope in them, plus some straw. And in at least one crate, pipe tobacco. What was going on?

Dexter left the rope on the box and made his way back through the musty kitchen. He saw what looked like a back door. The door opened easily, squeaking loudly. The steps to the backyard were rotted, and Dexter carefully made his way down them. They groaned under his weight.

Now he was at the back of the house, where overgrown weeds had taken over the yard. He climbed through a tangle of old sunflowers and finally stood away from the house. He looked back. The building seemed so old and worn, so neglected.

Something bright caught Dexter's eyes, something hidden in the forest of shrubbery lining the yard. Something bright red that shone like a piece of metal. He reached into the bushes and pulled back some branches. Now he could see that a driveway wide enough for a car or truck had been made on the other side of the bushes. He stared. In the driveway was a shiny, brand-new van, its windows sparkling clean, its silver chrome gleaming in the sun.

Dexter caught his breath and cautiously peeked in the rear window. He saw some splinters of wood and a big spool of rope, like the rope he had found in the house. That was all.

Where was the owner of the van? Suddenly Dexter felt uneasy. He moved away from the window, and the branches of the thick bushes snapped at him. He jumped. It was time to get out of there. Fast.

Dexter made his way around the house, pushing through the weeds, and found his bike.

As he cycled away from the old house, he took one last look. The house looked the same—old, falling apart, and uncared for—but now Dexter knew something was different.

Somebody was using the house. Had anyone been there when Dexter was? Had somebody been hiding in the basement while he roamed around upstairs, looking through every room? Dexter pedaled faster, wondering what the new van was doing there.

And the rope, the doughnuts, and the crates. And the *Random Review.*

When Dexter got home, he automatically reset his odometer, making a note that he had ridden exactly sixteen miles. He leaned his bike against the porch and raced over to the Temple house. He couldn't wait to tell Jay and Cindy about his discovery.

3 · *Mysterious Mummy's Mask*

THE TEMPLE KITCHEN looked exactly the way it had when Dexter left. Papers were strewn all over the table, and Jay and Cindy were working with rubber cement, a ruler, and scissors.

"Hi, Dex," said Jay, looking up. "Did you save the day with another ad?"

"I sure did," Dexter said, grinning. "I sold an ad to a hard-of-hearing woman, a Mrs. Campbell from Abe's Market, out on the country road."

Cindy looked pleased. "We're one terrific team, there's no doubt about it. Including Mom. She said she could type everything up in an hour.

Then all that will be left is a little cutting and pasting."

Dexter sat down at the table. "After I got the ad from Mrs. Campbell, I rode a little farther down the road. I knew I had extra time, and I wanted to get more miles on my bike, so I—"

"How many miles did you do today?" Jay asked.

"Sixteen, exactly, from this house to an old empty house and back here again," Dexter said.

He frowned. "There's something funny going on at that old house. At least it seems odd to me."

"Odd?" Cindy said, interested.

Dexter pushed his glasses up on his nose. "Well, it's an abandoned house—you've seen houses like that out in the country. Roof slanted, porch falling down, that sort of thing." He paused, remembering the sense of loneliness he had felt in the empty rooms.

"And?" Jay prodded.

"There was a brand-new van of some kind parked outside in the bushes, hidden," Dexter went on. "I'm sure it was hidden on purpose. I had the feeling that someone was using the house, or had used it. There were some big crates in one of the rooms and a new doughnut box with some fresh doughnuts in it. And believe it or not, a copy of last week's *Random Review.*" He shook his head.

"Maybe the van is stolen, and someone's trying to hide it until they can sneak it out of town," Jay suggested.

"And whoever stole the van is staying in the house until it's safe to leave," Cindy offered.

"What about the crates?" Dexter asked. "And there was a lot of rope around, too."

Jay frowned. "Maybe the crates were in the truck, and the guy just wanted to get rid of them."

Cindy started to laugh. "It's not enough that we have a newspaper to finish pasting up this afternoon. Now we have to dream up a mystery. After all, there's nothing mysterious about someone going in to look around an old house. You did. Maybe someone else will see your bicycle tracks and start dreaming up a mystery. And maybe someone will call the police, and the police will trace the bike to you. And maybe—"

Dexter shook his head. "I still think there's something funny going on. And I'm going to find out what it's all about. First chance I get, I'm riding back out there."

The telephone rang. "I'll get it," said Jay, jumping up.

The voice was familiar.

"Jay? This is Mr. Pruitt. I wonder if you and Dexter would do me a great favor and stop over here for a minute. I'd like to talk to you. And please bring your rake."

"Sure, Mr. Pruitt," Jay said, looking over at Dexter. "We'll be right there."

Jay hung up the phone. "Mr. Pruitt wants us to come over. He didn't say what for, except to bring a rake. Maybe we haven't lost that job after all!"

"Let's go," Dexter said, getting up from the table. "And then after we talk with him, I have to go downtown to the Bon Ton. I think I've talked them into placing a full-page ad for a sale they're going to have next week. A full-page ad would be like five ads in one!"

"Don't forget that the paste-up has to be at the printshop by five, Jay," Cindy reminded him. "I'll have everything ready."

The boys left and rode their bikes the two blocks over to Mr. Pruitt's house. Jay carried a rake over his shoulder.

At Mr. Pruitt's, they saw a truck parked across the street in front of the Sheldon house. The lettering on the side of the truck read "Lon's Lawn Service." A man in a bright orange shirt was slowly pushing a power mower across the Sheldon lawn. He stared at the boys as they parked their bikes and walked toward Mr. Pruitt's back door.

Jay knocked, and Mr. Pruitt answered the door. He smiled when he saw the boys, his forehead wrinkling.

"It was a mean trick I pulled, boys," he said. "Hiring a lawn service when you two have always done such a good job. I knew you were busy with your newspaper, and I thought I'd try out this new service. But look." He waved his hand at the lawn in front of him.

"The man they sent over, Hank, didn't even sweep up the grass he butchered. Maybe he was in too much of a hurry to get to his job there at the Sheldons' across the street. Anyway, I need your help. I should have known that nobody, not even a professional lawn service, could do as good a job as you two boys."

Jay and Dexter exchanged glances.

"Well, then," said Mr. Pruitt briskly, "how about raking and sweeping up for me? I'm expecting out-of-town company. They're spending the night, and tomorrow morning they'll be looking at my roses. Then I'm taking them over to see the museum. I'd like to have my place looking its best."

Jay spoke quickly. "Dexter has to run some errands, but I can stay and finish up."

"Thanks, men," Mr. Pruitt said. His forehead wrinkled again in a smile, and he closed the door.

"So much for Lon's Lawn Service," Dexter said with satisfaction. "We're the best, after all, just the way we've said all along."

"Try the rest, we're still the best," said Jay. "That could be our ad."

"I hate to leave you to do the job alone, but I've got to get downtown to the Bon Ton," said Dexter.

"There's not much to do, anyway," Jay told him. "It's more important for you to get some more ads. Why don't you try that Lon's Lawn Service? Maybe they'd put an ad in next week's issue."

"Good idea," said Dexter. "I'll go over and talk to that Hank person right now."

"Tell him we'll even write the copy for their ad," said Jay with a smile. "Leave it to Lon, they'll do it wrong."

Dexter laughed and walked across the street to Hank.

Hank had broad shoulders beneath his bright orange shirt, and his arms hung long next to his thick body. Maybe his arms look so long because he's slouching, Dexter thought. He introduced himself.

"Would you like to put an ad for Lon's Lawn Service in our paper?" Dexter asked. "We give the paper free to everyone in the Random Street neighborhood. And we leave lots of copies with our advertisers to give away. You might pick up some new customers."

The bulky man ran a dirt-streaked hand through his thick blond hair. "Ask the boss," he said curtly. "I've nothing to do with that end of the business. I just go where he tells me and cut the lawn. Lon's Lawn Service is Lon's business, not mine, kid."

He turned back to the lawn mower.

Dexter reached into his pocket for a folded copy of the most recent *Random Review.*

"Would you mind showing this to your boss?" he asked. "He might want to put an ad in next week's issue. It's too late for this week—we have to get the copy over to the printer this afternoon."

The man made no move to take the paper, and finally Dexter said, "We have a special five-time rate. I'll just put this copy here on the front seat of your pickup, okay?"

Hank shrugged, his heavy-lidded eyes not looking at Dexter. Maybe he wouldn't show the paper to his boss, Dexter thought. He copied the telephone number of Lon's Lawn Service from the lettering on the side of the pickup. He'd call Lon later this afternoon and make an appointment.

Dexter got back on his bike and started to cycle downtown to the Bon Ton.

Jay saw Dexter and waved. He was raking Mr. Pruitt's cut grass in long sweeps. It did seem as if Hank had done a sloppy job, Jay thought. He glanced across the street. Hank was watching him.

Jay suddenly felt sorry for Hank. He must

have realized he'd done a bad job, especially now that Jay was finishing up what Hank should have done himself. Maybe he was afraid that Mr. Pruitt would complain to Lon. Maybe he thought he'd lose his job. Jay looked over again at the man. Hank wasn't even working now, just leaning on his lawn mower. How could he expect to keep any lawn jobs if he just stood around?

Jay shrugged and kept raking. Mr. Pruitt's praise had certainly made him feel good. He wanted to do an extra neat job. On an impulse, he decided he'd clean out the wells of the basement windows. He'd been meaning to before, but he'd never really had the time.

He gathered all the piles of grass together and put them in a lawn bag he'd taken from the supply in Mr. Pruitt's garage. The window wells were at the far end of the house, heavily shaded by the big maple trees in the yard. The leaves had been piling up for weeks now, so the wells were nearly full.

Jay brought his bag over and started stuffing it with the leaves and twigs from one of the wells. After more than a dozen armfuls, the first well was finished. Jay sat back on his heels and wiped his forehead. The maple trees made this end of the yard cool and dark, but he was hot from his work. A breeze moved the heavy branches above Jay. The shadows played against the side of the house, making eerie figures out of splotches of sun.

Jay crawled over to the next well, dragging the bag with him. It seemed ten times quieter back here than in the front of the house. The yard was almost silent, except for the slight creaking of the heavy branches in the wind.

The next window well was packed with leaves. Jay dug in and again started hauling out armfuls of leaves and twigs. Reach in, grab, haul out. His fingers were used to the feel of the leaves and twigs, and he had built a pretty smooth rhythm. He'd be finished in no time.

Suddenly Jay's fingers closed around something different. Something that was soft and large, almost as big as a football. Jay nearly dropped the object back into the well, he was so surprised. He bent over, closer to the well, and peered at the thing he held in his hands.

He frowned. There was something hard beneath a white, thick cloth. Funny. The cloth certainly wasn't dirty or stained. It couldn't have been outdoors in the well very long. He tested the weight of the object. Whatever was wrapped inside the white cloth was pretty heavy.

Slowly Jay began to unwind the thick wrapping. He peeled off layer after layer, his curiosity mounting. What could be inside? He gently pulled the last of the cloth away. And suddenly he was staring into a strange face, a golden face with bright green eyes.

Green eyes that stared back at him, unblinking.

Jay couldn't take his eyes away from that beautiful golden face with the green eyes sparkling in the sun.

He shook his head in wonder and surprise. He'd never held anything like this before, never in his life.

He wondered how on earth the face got here, in Mr. Pruitt's window well, all covered with leaves.

He turned the object over and over in his hands, rubbing it gently with his fingers.

The face was really a mask made of heavy metal of some kind, smooth as the smoothest stone he had ever felt. Jay's heart pounded. Was the

metal bronze? Gold? Something clicked in his mind. He remembered something he had seen on a field trip with his class.

A mummy's mask. That was it. An ancient Egyptian mummy's mask.

4 • A Dark, Empty House

JAY STOOD UP quickly. He'd have to show the mummy's mask to Mr. Pruitt. He couldn't wait to tell Dexter and Cindy. They wouldn't believe it. He could hardly believe it himself.

He hurriedly wrapped the mask in the cloth and ran to Mr. Pruitt's front door. He noticed that the man in the orange shirt, Hank, was still across the street, watching him.

"Done already?" asked Mr. Pruitt when he opened the door. "I can promise that you and your friend Dexter are in for a terrific bonus when Christmastime finally rolls around."

Without saying anything, Jay held up the mask, still wrapped in the cloth.

Mr. Pruitt blinked and stepped back. "What's that?" he asked.

Jay tried to tell him. "I found it in one of your window wells, Mr. Pruitt. Look!" He unwrapped the cloth and produced the golden mask for Mr. Pruitt to see.

"It's a mummy's mask, Mr. Pruitt. An Egyptian mummy's mask."

Mr. Pruitt took the mask from Jay's hands and stared at it. "Why, this is—this is incredible," he whispered.

"I thought it was pretty neat myself," Jay said, feeling a twinge of pride at having found the mask. "I can't think why it would be in your window well," he went on. "Should we call the police?"

Still staring at the mask, Mr. Pruitt waved his hand at Jay. "I'll take care of everything. Just leave it to me. It's quite extraordinary." He started to close the door.

"But shouldn't we do something about it?" Jay

insisted. "Shouldn't we at least put something about the mask in our paper, the *Random Review*?" He felt frustrated. He wanted to talk more about the mask.

"Fine, fine," Mr. Pruitt said impatiently, shutting the door on Jay.

Well, at least the Spotlighters could put the story in their paper. What a story! Jay was still standing on the porch when he heard someone call his name.

"Jay!" It was Cindy. "Do you want me to run the copy over to the printer?"

"Hold the presses!" Jay called back. "I've got the front-page story of the summer!"

He dashed down the sidewalk toward Cindy, forgetting about his rake and bag of clippings. He dashed past Hank, who was still leaning against his lawn mower.

"The mystery of the mummy's mask!" said Cindy when Jay told her what had happened. "Let's figure out the story right away."

As soon as they were sitting at the kitchen table, Cindy scribbled on a note pad. "I'll take out this story about the dog pound and use it next week," she decided out loud. "Then the mask story can be right on the front page." She tapped her pencil on the paper. "Tell me again exactly what the mask looked like."

Jay leaned forward. "First of all, it was covered by layers and layers of a thick, white cloth. The cloth wasn't dirty or anything, so somebody must have just wrapped up the mask. I was really surprised when I finally unwound it. The face had the greenest eyes and—"

"Emeralds, maybe?" Cindy suggested.

"I don't know," Jay admitted. "But they were awfully green and bright. And the rest of the face was gold. It was beautiful. And very heavy. Not like a regular old Halloween mask, you know, but solid."

Cindy nodded, trying to sketch what Jay was explaining.

"You went on that same field trip I did, didn't you?" Jay asked. "That one at the museum with all the Egyptian stuff and everything? This mask was like an ancient Egyptian mummy's mask. I'm sure it's really valuable."

Jay rested his chin in his hands. "I wonder

what Mr. Pruitt is going to do with it. I wonder if he'll call the police."

"I wonder, too," Cindy mused, jotting notes. "How about this for our front-page story? 'A curious object was discovered in the yard of Mr. Amos Pruitt, of Corrigan Way. At first glance the object appeared to be a metal face, but on closer examination it proved to be a relic of the ancient past: a gold mummy's mask. At this time, no one has any clues as to how the valuable mask came to be in a yard in the Random Street neighborhood. New facts will be reported in this paper as they are discovered by your reporter.' "

Jay reached across the table to read what Cindy had written. "Where's my name?" he demanded. "I was the one who found the mummy's mask."

"We don't put our own names in the paper," Cindy explained. "I didn't put in mine. I just wrote 'your reporter.' That's what you're supposed to do when you write an article for a newspaper. Otherwise it looks as if you're bragging."

"Big deal," Jay said. "And I was the one who made the discovery."

"I know," said Cindy. "But it's more professional this way. Trust me."

Within an hour, Mrs. Temple had typed up the new copy, and Jay had everything ready for the printer.

"Aha!" said Mr. Waller when Jay walked into Instantly Yours, the printshop. "One Jay Temple and one paste-up of the *Random Review.* Am I right?"

"You're right," Jay said, smiling. He sat on one of the stools in front of the counter and helped himself to a piece of candy from a dish.

"I was just going to close up shop," said Mr. Waller. "So I'm glad to have the paste-up. I can start working on it first thing in the morning, before you kids are stirring. I'm an early bird, you know, up at the crack of dawn. You can probably pick up your papers long before noon."

"That will be great," Jay told him. "Then we can deliver them early."

"How do you deliver them?" asked Mr. Waller. "Carrier pigeon, perhaps?"

Jay unwrapped another piece of candy. "Yep, in a way. Dexter and Cindy and I are the carrier pigeons. We each take certain blocks and carry the papers on our bikes. It only takes us an hour or so. We put stacks of papers all over town, in stores and in places like the Southport Cinema. I figure everyone in Kenoska sees the *Random Review.*"

Mr. Waller took the paste-up out of the envelope and glanced at it.

"I like your joke," he said, laughing. "Very, very funny."

"Thanks," said Jay. "Actually, it's one you told me a couple of weeks ago."

"So it is," said Mr. Waller. "Well, if a joke's worth laughing at once, it's worth laughing at twice."

Suddenly he bent his head over the copy and uttered a smothered exclamation. Then he ran his fingers through his hair and looked at Jay. "An odd story, here," he said finally.

"Isn't it exciting?" Jay said. He told Mr. Waller the details of finding the mummy's mask.

"And that's why I was almost late," Jay explained. "We wanted to include a story about the mask in the paper."

"So you found the mask," said Mr. Waller. He

coughed. "In Mr. Pruitt's window well," he said, recovering.

Jay nodded eagerly. "At first I didn't know what it was. A face made of metal, with green eyes—green glass, maybe, or precious stones."

"Pruitt would know," Mr. Waller said evenly. "He's connected with the Gilliland Museum." Mr. Waller glanced up at Jay and then back at the story. "And Pruitt took the mask into his house," he said slowly. "Does he still have it?"

"I don't know," Jay admitted. "All of this happened just a couple of hours ago." He thought for a moment. "Mr. Pruitt was expecting guests, and they were going to stay overnight," he remembered. "Maybe he hasn't had time to do anything about the mask."

Mr. Waller glanced at the clock. "So," he said, "has he called the police?"

"I suppose so," said Jay. "I'm not sure."

Mr. Waller caught his lower lip in his teeth and made a sucking noise. He looked at his watch and then back at the clock. "Closing time," he said, turning his back to Jay and walking over to the telephone.

"Oh, sure," said Jay, sliding off the stool. "What time do you think we can pick up the papers tomorrow?"

"I'll call you," said Mr. Waller. "I'll call you when they're ready."

As Jay closed the door to the printshop, he looked back. Mr. Waller was already speaking into the telephone.

Was he calling Mr. Pruitt? Jay wondered. Or the police?

"Who's ready to celebrate the fourth issue of the *Random Review*?" Mrs. Temple asked when Jay got back from Instantly Yours. "How about going to the Spaghetti Factory for supper and then seeing a movie afterwards? My treat for you two and Dexter. And myself, of course."

"Great!" Cindy and Jay said together.

"Where is Dexter, anyway?" Mrs. Temple asked, glancing at the clock.

"Oh, I saw him on my way back from the printer," Jay said. "He spent a million years at the Bon Ton and got them to sign up for a full-page ad for next week."

"A double celebration, then!" Mrs. Temple said. "Call him and tell him to come on over."

"I already told him to come over," Jay said, with a grin. "I wanted to tell him about the mask. He'll be here any minute."

As soon as Dexter arrived, they all piled into Mrs. Temple's car and drove to the Spaghetti Factory restaurant. When they were seated and had given the waitress their orders, Dexter turned to Jay. "Now tell me about that mask. Tell me everything."

Jay filled him in on what he had found and what they had written in the *Random Review* for tomorrow's edition.

"Maybe the mask is a fake," suggested Dexter.

"But even if it is, what was it doing in Mr. Pruitt's window well?" asked Cindy. "And the cloth wasn't even damp. It had probably only been there a day or two."

"I'm sure that mask isn't a fake," said Jay confidently. "You should have seen it. And Mr. Pruitt seemed pretty excited—he's probably called the police by now."

"If the mummy's mask is real, it must have been stolen from a museum," said Cindy.

Mrs. Temple shook her head. "Not necessarily. Someone could have stolen it at the site of an excavation. Some of those beautiful ancient things never get to the museum where they're supposed to go. They're stolen first. For example, one of the workers might steal a valuable vase right while the digging is going on. Then he sells it for very little money to someone in another city who knows where he can sell it for more money. And so on up the chain, through dealer after dealer, until that vase ends up in the hands of an unscrupulous collector who is willing to pay a fortune for it."

"What does *unscrupulous* mean?" asked Jay.

"Someone without scruples," Dexter explained. "Scruples are what tell you whether something is right or wrong and make you do what's right."

Mrs. Temple nodded. "And being unscrupulous is knowing something's wrong, inside and out, but doing it anyway."

"Unscrupulous," said Jay. "I'm glad I don't have to say it three times in a row, fast."

The waitress brought four plates of steaming spaghetti.

"That looks terrific," said Dexter. "I'm starved."

"Thieves have to trust each other," Mrs. Temple went on. "The collector knows that the objects have been stolen, but he also knows that they are not fakes. He trusts the crook he is dealing with because the thief has a reputation."

"For being a crook?" asked Dexter, twirling a forkful of spaghetti.

"Yes, but also for selling truly ancient art, not fakes. If he sold just one fake, word would spread and he would be finished. No one would ever buy from him again."

"There must be lots of valuable things in some of those old tombs," said Dexter.

"It's because kings and queens and rich people thought they could take their possessions with them after they died," said Cindy.

Dexter tore a piece of garlic bread from a hot loaf in a covered basket. "I still don't understand how the mask got to Mr. Pruitt's window well," he said.

"Wait!" said Cindy suddenly.

Dexter paused, his bread halfway to his mouth.

"Mr. Pruitt," she went on, nearly tipping over her water glass in her excitement. "Let's say Mr. Pruitt secretly wanted to buy the mummy's mask. He had someone drop it off at his house at night. That way no one would see Mr. Pruitt and the dealer together. Then Mr. Pruitt could sneak the mask out from their prearranged hiding place in the window well. And then he could—"

She stopped.

"Mr. Pruitt!" Dexter and Jay spoke at once, shocked.

Jay shook his head. "You've got to be crazy, Cindy, to suspect him. We've known him for ages."

Mrs. Temple smiled. "I think that's pretty unlikely, dear."

"Well, he could have," said Cindy defensively. "It wouldn't be the first time we've thought someone was nice and then found out the person was a crook."

"Cindy's right, really," said Jay. "Not about Mr. Pruitt, but about our having to suspect everyone."

"Even me, I suppose," suggested Mrs. Temple.

"You're first on the list," Dexter assured her.

"Speaking of lists," said Jay, "there's a list of desserts on the menu. How about chocolate cream pie with whipped cream or maybe a butterscotch double-decker sundae?"

They ordered desserts and finished their dinners. Soon they were all on their way to the movie.

They could talk more tomorrow, Cindy decided, as they walked into the theater. She was probably silly to suspect that Mr. Pruitt could be involved in stealing a piece of art like a mummy's mask.

After the movie, the Temples dropped Dexter off at his house. It was almost eleven o'clock.

"I'm even too sleepy to talk about the movie," Cindy said, heading upstairs to her bedroom. "See you in the morning, Jay."

"Night," Jay said. He felt pretty tired himself. It had been a long day, what with getting the *Random Review* ready, finding the mummy's mask, trying to figure out the mystery, and—

Jay slapped his hand against his forehead. In all the excitement of finding the mask, he had never finished cleaning up at Mr. Pruitt's! He'd left that big bag of clippings and the rake leaning against the house. And Mr. Pruitt had said how important it was for the yard to look nice for his company. Jay groaned. It was late, but he'd have to go over to Pruitt's now.

Quietly he went downstairs and hurried down Random Street to Corrigan Way. The streetlight on the corner swayed in the cool summer breeze. There wasn't another person on the street.

Jay reached Mr. Pruitt's house and stopped. There was the rake, right where he had left it. He hurried across the dark lawn to the back of the house. He fumbled around on the ground for the lawn bag—it was so dark he could hardly see. There. He grabbed the bag and stood up.

Suddenly Jay stopped. It was very dark—too dark. He realized that he hadn't seen any lights in Mr. Pruitt's house. Not even the porch light was turned on. If Mr. Pruitt had company, why was the house dark? It wasn't that late. Frowning, Jay carried the lawn bag to the garage. Then he returned to the front of the house and took his rake, glancing back at the house as he headed across the lawn to the street.

Something else was odd. Mr. Pruitt's car was not in his driveway. Everything was quiet, empty, and dark. The wind creaked through the branches of the trees in the yard, and Jay spun around. There was nothing there. He was alone, but . . .

Holding his rake over his shoulder, Jay ran back down Corrigan Way to his own street. He hurriedly put the rake in the garage and went inside the Temple house. He was out of breath, even though he hadn't run that far. He'd have to wait until morning to tell Dexter and Cindy about Mr. Pruitt's strange, dark, empty house.

5 • *Break-in!*

DEXTER CAME OVER to the Temple house at ten o'clock the next morning.

"Has Mr. Waller called yet?" he asked Cindy.

"Not yet," Cindy answered. She glanced at the clock. "Why don't we ride over there and save him the phone call?" she suggested. "Besides, I can hardly wait to see the paper in print."

"Good idea," Dexter said. The Spotlighters left the house and headed their bikes toward Mr. Waller's printshop.

"Wait till I tell you about last night," said Jay, as they pedaled.

"I was there, remember," Dexter reminded him. "Spaghetti Factory, movie, and all."

"No, after that. I went over to Mr. Pruitt's to pick up the lawn bag and the rake. I'd forgotten them. I knew he'd be mad because he was going to have guests, and the guests were going to be looking around at his rose bushes this morning before seeing the museum."

Dexter groaned. "We just got him back as a customer, and now we'll lose him again."

Jay shook his head. "He wasn't there. The house was locked tight, his car was gone, the lights were off. And early this morning I rode over to see if he was back and there still wasn't a sign of anyone."

"But he was expecting guests," said Dexter, pushing his glasses up on his nose.

"That's what he told us," said Jay. "It looks as if he changed his plans."

Cindy took a breath. "I told you there was something funny about Mr. Pruitt."

The Spotlighters reached Instantly Yours and parked their bikes. Still talking, they pushed open the front door.

Then they suddenly stopped, their eyes wide.

Papers and boxes were strewn everywhere. Drawers were dumped out, shelves upturned.

Speechless, they stared.

Mr. Waller appeared from behind one of the printing presses. "What happened?" Dexter asked.

Mr. Waller shrugged his shoulders and looked around at the mess. "Someone broke into the shop last night," he said.

"Was anything valuable taken—like money or equipment?" Cindy asked.

"No, as a matter of fact," Mr. Waller said. "I've checked everything out. Things are just messed up, that's all."

"Why would anyone do this?" Jay asked, shaking his head.

Mr. Waller stared at the floor, silent.

"Did you call the police?" Dexter asked, straightening.

"No need to do that," Mr. Waller said briskly. "Nothing was stolen. It was probably just a prank. The police couldn't do anything about it anyway." He looked once more around the room and then at the Spotlighters.

"There is one thing, though," he said, clearing his throat.

Jay, Cindy, and Dexter looked at him.

"The paste-up of your *Random Review* is missing."

"The paste-up is missing?" asked Cindy, her voice rising.

Mr. Waller nodded. "I knew how much it meant to you kids to have the paper ready this morning, so I was going to run it through in spite of everything." He looked over the piles of papers on the floor. "But the paste-up isn't anywhere. I've searched from top to bottom. Whoever broke in must have taken it."

He cleared his throat again. "I can't understand why anyone would want your paste-up. Think you can redo it?"

Cindy thought quickly. How long would it take to rewrite this week's issue and paste it up? They'd have to start all over from scratch. It was impossible. The *Random Review* could not be delivered this week.

"We'll have to skip this week," Cindy said. "I didn't even keep a copy of what we wrote."

Mr. Waller's shoulders rose and fell. "Sorry about that," he said. "Wish I could help."

"Speaking of helping," Jay said. "Can we help you straighten up this mess? We've got plenty of time now that we can't deliver our paper."

Mr. Waller shook his head and smiled. "Thanks, but I've got a crew coming in to take care of things." He looked around the shop and sighed. The telephone rang, and he went to answer it.

"See you later," Jay said as the Spotlighters left the shop.

Cindy was angry and disappointed about the paper. They'd worked so hard. But more than that, she was mystified. Why would anyone steal the paste-up of the *Random Review*? It must have been a mistake.

The Spotlighters headed home.

"I don't get it," said Jay. "Who would want the paste-up besides us?"

"They probably took that envelope thinking it was something else," Dexter said. "That's exactly what happened on a TV show last week. The robber didn't realize he had the wrong package until it was too late. And then—"

Jay interrupted. "Or maybe they stole that envelope to cover up what they really took. But we don't know what that was."

Dexter nodded. "There was a program like that, too," he said. "And the plan worked. Nobody guessed what it was the thieves were really after. I guess as long as something—anything—is stolen, that's what everyone thinks the thief is looking for."

Cindy nodded slowly. "That must be the answer, because no one would bother stealing our paper."

"Nope," said Jay. "My jokes are good, but not that good. No, there's no one who could have wanted the paste-up and no one who'd want to keep the paper from being printed."

Dexter pushed his glasses up. "I know! A rival newspaper. They're going to come out with something called *Random Razzmatazz* or *Randomly Yours*. They want to make us look silly. After all, our readers are looking forward to tomorrow's issue. And our advertisers have paid money for their ads."

Jay groaned. "And now we'll have to return that money. Why did I say I'd be bookkeeper? I'll be doing nothing all week but trying to figure out the budget. Balancing books is as hard for me as balancing a banana on my nose."

"We've spent some of that money on new supplies," Cindy said glumly. "We won't even be able to pay all the advertisers back."

"Our reputations are ruined," said Jay. "Who wants a sandwich? Eating will calm our nerves."

"Thinking calms mine," said Cindy.

"Let's do both," suggested Dexter.

They pedaled home.

While they ate their sandwiches, they talked about the missing newspaper. "I'll go around and tell our advertisers," said Dexter, patting his back pocket. "Luckily I have a list. I'll explain everything. If they want to have an ad in next week's issue, they can have it for free."

"Cindy and I can stay here and figure out next week's paper," suggested Jay. "We can use some of the stuff we remember from this issue. My joke, for instance, and the story about the mummy's mask."

Dexter stretched. "I'll see how many miles I can put on my odometer today," he told them. "Maybe by Saturday I'll have finished three hundred. Then I can get my T-shirt."

Soon Dexter was on his way, stopping to talk with anyone who had placed an ad in this week's *Random Review*. After a couple of hours, he checked his list. He had only one more advertiser to see—Mrs. Campbell out at Abe's Market. So far, everyone had been very nice about the cancelled paper. He knew Mrs. Campbell would be, too. After all, the robbery hadn't been his fault or Jay's or Cindy's. How mean of someone to take their paste-up! All their hard work, all for nothing. He wondered what the thief thought he was getting instead of a newspaper paste-up. Someone sure would be surprised and disappointed to find he'd stolen the *Random Review*.

Dexter shook his head. How could anyone have made such a mistake? Cindy had printed big black letters on the envelope: "Paste-up for *Random Review*."

Had the paper really been taken by accident?

Dexter pedaled on steadily, his mind on the break-in. Had someone really wanted to steal the paste-up of the *Random Review*?

But why would someone want to make sure the *Random Review* wasn't printed and distributed?

He tried to think. What was in the paper? The story about the mummy's mask! Was there anyone who wouldn't want that story circulated?

Maybe there was someone. Maybe the person who had hidden the mask in Mr. Pruitt's window well.

Dexter shook his head. But there was no way the story could be kept secret. Probably Mr. Pruitt had already called the police.

Besides, the next issue of the *Random Review* would carry the same story.

Dexter concentrated. Maybe next week it wouldn't matter. Maybe it was important to some-one that the story not be read today. Not be read—by whom?

Who wouldn't want the story about the mask to be printed? It seemed impossible to figure out. Almost everyone in Kenoska read the *Random Review*. Why, he'd even seen a copy in that old farmhouse—

The old farmhouse! Could there be some kind of answer there? But what? Dexter pedaled harder and faster.

He thought about the signs of recent activity

and the feeling he had had yesterday that whoever owned the red van did not want it to be discovered.

He remembered the discussion the night before at the Spaghetti Factory about thieves stealing ancient objects. Could that be what was going on at the old farmhouse? What about those crates? Something had been packed in them. Were stolen objects being taken there and then sold?

How could it all be connected with the story of the mummy's mask in the *Random Review*?

He decided to go back to the farmhouse. Maybe there was some clue there, after all. It was worth taking another look.

In his excitement, Dexter almost passed the driveway to the old farmhouse. He stared down the long, overgrown stretch of driveway for the second time in two days.

There were more tire tracks this time. Curious, he pedaled toward the old house. So far everything looked the same. The same old sagging porch, the same rotted swing. Dexter rode around to the left of the house where overgrown bushes spilled into the yard. He braked, got off his bike, and put the kickstand down.

What if someone was here? Dexter put one foot carefully in front of the other and made his way quietly to the back of the house. As he turned the corner, his bike tipped over into the bushes. The sound startled him, and he jumped. When he reached the backyard, Dexter stopped dead in his tracks. Parked close to the bushes was Lon's Lawn Service truck. What was that truck doing here?

Dexter's heart pounded. He was onto something, something big. Something scary.

Hank was here. Hank, the lazy man who had done such a poor job with Mr. Pruitt's lawn. It was Hank who had seen Jay with the mask at Mr. Pruitt's. And Dexter had talked to Hank about the newspaper. Hank knew the paper was going to be printed in the morning. And he'd guessed the story would be in the paper.

It had to be Hank who had broken into Mr. Waller's printshop.

Suddenly Dexter knew he couldn't handle this alone. He'd have to get out of here. Fast. He'd head back home, back to Jay and Cindy. Maybe the police.

Just as Dexter turned around, he thought he heard someone behind him. And before he could react, there was a stabbing pain at the back of his neck. Something hard had hit him. Then everything went dark. Dexter collapsed in a heap in the bushes.

6 • Dexter Held Prisoner

COMING TO, Dexter had no idea how much time had passed. All he knew was that his head ached and he could barely move. He struggled to pull himself up, then realized with horror that he was bound securely with heavy cord.

He squinted and blinked, trying to see in the dimness. And then he realized something else. His glasses were gone! They must have fallen off when he was knocked out. His heart throbbed, and he thought he could hear the blood pounding in his head.

Relax, he told himself. But that was almost impossible. He was tied up with rope—the same rope he had seen in the back of the van yesterday? Probably. And where was he? He strained his eyes, trying to see what was around him. But everything was blurry and misshapen. He blinked furiously, thinking he smelled sawdust. And something else. Pipe tobacco.

Suddenly Dexter knew where he was, tied and bound. In a wooden crate, like the ones he had seen yesterday.

He felt uncomfortably warm and wished stupidly that he had worn a short-sleeved shirt and shorts. But if he had, he reminded himself, he would probably feel the rope biting into his skin even more. He struggled again, trying to find a loose end. There was none.

All of a sudden Dexter stiffened. He could hear floorboards groaning softly under someone's feet.

The footsteps drew closer and closer to Dexter's prison.

Whose footsteps were they, anyway? All at once Dexter relaxed. Jay and Cindy. They'd come to rescue him. And then, as quickly as the thought had come, he realized that Jay and Cindy couldn't be here. They had no idea where he was. No one knew.

Dexter didn't know whether to yell or keep quiet.

The footsteps came closer and closer. Friend or enemy? Dexter tensed, his eyes wide.

He heard a door open, very close by.

And now someone stood next to the crate, next to him. The lid was yanked off. Dexter blinked.

A face loomed large above him. He squinted, trying to see. And as the face drew closer, Dexter instinctively ducked, trying to shield himself from another blow.

"Don't worry, I won't hurt you," said a husky voice.

Hank. It was Hank's voice. Then it must have been Hank who had knocked him out, tied him up, and put him in this crate.

Except for his pounding heart, Dexter was silent.

"I had to keep you quiet, you understand?" Hank asked, bending over Dexter.

"You could get me into real big-time trouble," Hank told him, "if you open your mouth about what you've seen out here. Or about that mask that your friend found." He paused. "You think you understand?"

He seemed to be waiting for Dexter to say something. Dexter nodded. He did understand.

He wanted to ask Hank to loosen the ropes on his legs and arms, but he kept silent.

"I don't know the whole story about all this

stuff," Hank said. He fumbled in his pocket for something and took out a pack of cigarettes and some matches.

Dexter swallowed. Hank's not the pipe-smoker, he thought.

Hank lit a cigarette and blew the smoke out over Dexter's head. "I was hired to bring boxes from another place not far from here, you see? They just hired me to do that, nothing more, just bring boxes here. They didn't tell me anything about what was in those boxes." He took another puff on his cigarette and went on. "Stolen goods, I figured. Why else would they hire me to move the boxes at night? Especially to an old dump like this. The woman owns this house, and she thinks no one ever comes out here."

Dexter felt stiff. He shifted his position a little, and Hank's eyes narrowed.

"I'm not untying you, just remember that. And there's no way you can wiggle out of that rope. I've got to keep you under cover. Under *this* cover," he added, tapping the lid to the crate.

"Just so you understand the whole picture," he went on. "So you know why you better keep still as a mouse, no matter what happens. No matter what."

Hank pinched his cigarette and let the dead ashes fall to the floor.

"I was sure I was transporting stolen goods. Maybe something really valuable, worth a heap. So what would it hurt if I sneaked one of the things from a crate? They had so much, they'd never miss one thing."

Dexter's heart thudded against his ribs. That was it. Hank had stolen the mummy's mask. Stolen the mask from the thieves themselves.

"I took something. A kind of mask. I stuck it in my pickup. But I couldn't leave it there. If these characters ever suspected I'd stolen anything from them—"

He drew his hand across his throat.

"So I hid the mask in the window well, where your pal found it. I was going to get it later, after the bosses had left town." He brushed a strand of dirty blond hair from his forehead.

Dexter's head still ached, and his body felt sore all over. He wanted to stretch, to walk, to run. How he wished he could be on his bike right now, cycling away from this farmhouse, from Hank, from the danger ahead!

Hank's bosses had gotten hold of a lot of stolen objects—ancient, beautiful things like the mask that Jay had found. They knew the objects were valuable and could be sold to unscrupulous collectors. Hank had stolen the mask from his bosses. And now Hank was afraid they'd find out what he had done.

Hank leaned closer. "The whole operation is over tonight. They'll be leaving. They'll never see me again, I'll never see them. I don't even know their real names. They'll be okay, they'll be in Europe, they'll be rich. And I'll be okay, see? I'll be okay if no one finds out about you. Or the mask."

He kicked the crate in disgust. "How was I to know they had an inventory of everything? And tonight's their final inventory. They've got lists and lists. I can just hope they don't find out that the mask is missing. And if they do find out, they'd better not suspect I took it." He pulled at his ear. "You think I could have risked letting them read about a mysterious mummy's mask some dopey kids found in a window well? They'd put two and two together and point their ugly fingers at me."

Hank stood up, stretching. "If they'd seen the article about the mask in your paper, they'd have known. And they do read that dumb *Random Review*—they like to keep track of what's going on. So I had to stop the paper from being printed. I had to break into that printshop and search through all the stuff in there—"

He stopped, raising his thick arms over his head. "You've got to stay right where you are until it's all over. If they see you—if you so much as sneeze tonight when they're here, you might as well forget your name. They'll be in the next room. They'll never come in here unless they hear something funny."

Hank reached for the lid and started to replace it. "And don't think you can get loose from that rope," he said. "You can't."

Hank gave a short, mirthless laugh. "Oh, don't worry," he said, fitting the lid securely over Dexter's head. "I'll let you out, once this is all over. But not until I'm sure I'm in the clear. Remember that."

Dexter heard Hank's footsteps move away.

The boards creaked, and then there was silence. In a few minutes a truck started up. Hank was leaving.

Dexter pushed against the ropes. He had to get out. He had to get the police. The more he struggled against the tight ropes, the hotter he got. Desperately, Dexter kicked as hard as he could, feeling the pressure of the rope cut into his leg. But he had loosened something, he could feel it. Maybe it wasn't very much, but it was a start.

Beads of sweat rolled down Dexter's forehead as he worked against the ropes. He discovered that if he pushed steadily and slowly, he made some progress. He rested for a moment and then began again. Was he getting anywhere? He felt trapped, helpless, alone. Had an hour passed? Two? He had no idea.

Suddenly Dexter tensed, listening. A car was coming. Hank? He heard a car door slam and several voices. It must be the bosses, as Hank called them.

Dexter lay motionless in his small prison, hardly daring to breathe. The voices came closer. One was a woman's voice, and one a man's. Again

Dexter smelled tobacco. Somebody was smoking a pipe. It was the person who had been here before, then. The leader of the gang?

Dexter closed his eyes, his face hot. He wouldn't cough or sneeze if he could help it, or even move, except to try to loosen the twine. If he could silently work himself loose, he would find a way to escape. He would.

But the ropes were like a huge spider web, tough and strong. At last Dexter stopped struggling. He knew he was trapped.

7 • *Detective Work*

"WHERE'S DEX all this time, do you think?" asked Cindy, chewing her pencil. "He should have been back ages ago."

Mrs. Temple had an evening meeting, and Jay and Cindy had finished supper. Jay glanced at the kitchen clock. "Maybe he decided to finish up his three-hundred-mile stint and get his T-shirt so we could put the news in the paper. 'Random Street kid goes three hundred miles, gets T-shirt, but can't have his name in newspaper since he's one of the owners.' " He paused. "I still think my name should be in the story about the mummy's mask."

Cindy shook her head. "You're an egotist," she said.

"A what-o-tist?" asked Jay.

"Egotist. Someone who knows all kinds of good things about himself that nobody else knows."

Jay laughed and got up to peer into the refrigerator. He came back to the table with a bowl of grapes. "I still think it's mysterious about the paste-up being stolen from Mr. Waller's," he said.

"So do I," said Cindy. "I put *'Random Review'* in such big letters on the envelope that no one could possibly have taken it by accident."

Jay popped a grape into his mouth and chewed it thoughtfully. "Maybe the thief really wanted that issue of the *Random Review*," he said after a moment. "After all, nothing else important was missing, according to Mr. Waller. Maybe whoever had broken in didn't want our paper to be printed. Maybe he didn't want anyone to see it."

Cindy tapped her pencil thoughtfully. "Maybe there was something in the paper that someone didn't want us to publish."

Jay took another grape. "Maybe we wrote something that was dangerous. Dangerous to someone if a certain party read it."

Cindy shook her head. "But no one but us

knew what was going to be in the paper. And, anyway, everyone knows we'll put out another paper, telling the same news, saying the same things. No one could break into Mr. Waller's every single week the night before the paper was to be printed."

"Maybe someone just wanted to delay printing that *Random Review*," said Jay. "Maybe it wouldn't make any difference to the person if the news came out a week later."

Cindy sat forward. "The mummy's mask," she whispered. "Did you tell Mr. Pruitt you were going to put that story in the paper?"

Jay shut his eyes, trying to remember. "Yes, I think I did, but he didn't say anything. I mean, if he hadn't wanted us to put the story in, he'd have said something, wouldn't he?"

He rubbed his head. "You mean you really think it's possible that Mr. Pruitt knew about the mummy's mask—knew it was there in his window well?" He shook his head. "But he wouldn't have hidden the mask in his own window well unless he meant for someone to come for it later—someone who knew where the mask would be buried."

"But why?" asked Cindy. "Why would Mr. Pruitt bother to bury the mask? Why wouldn't he just give it to someone, if that's what he wanted to do?"

"So no one would connect Mr. Pruitt with the other person, the thief," explained Jay. He sat down. "Why am I talking like this? Mr. Pruitt couldn't be involved in anything. If he is, I hate being a detective."

"Lots of people we've liked have turned out to be crooks," Cindy reminded him. "Do you think Mr. Pruitt was really surprised when you showed him the mask? Maybe he was secretly mad that you'd found it."

Jay shook his head. "I don't know. He seemed surprised. But I don't think he wanted to call the police. Maybe someone *had* left the mask there for him to find."

He took another grape. "I don't know why I even started suspecting there was something suspicious about Mr. Pruitt. I guess because my mind plays tricks on me when I'm hungry." He looked up at the clock. "I wish Dexter would hurry."

"Maybe Dexter went over to Instantly Yours to

talk to Mr. Waller about something," suggested Cindy. "He was going to see all of our advertisers, remember?"

"Let's call and find out," said Jay, reaching for the telephone. "I know the Instantly Yours number by heart."

In a moment he heard Mr. Waller's voice.

"Mr. Waller, this is Jay Temple. Have you seen Dexter Tate? He's late and we were just wondering where he might be."

"Not here," Mr. Waller said. "I haven't seen him. Now let me ask you about another missing person—Mr. Pruitt. I know you do his lawn. He was supposed to drop off his usual copy for the museum bulletin today, but he hasn't. What's more, he doesn't answer his phone. That means the bulletin gets printed without his report—if the bulletin's going to be printed on time."

Jay frowned. Then Mr. Pruitt was still gone. Where could he be?

Mr. Waller went on. "When you brought in your paste-up yesterday with that front page story about the mummy's mask, I thought maybe you shouldn't run it in the *Random Review*. I thought

Mr. Pruitt would probably want the story in the museum bulletin, seeing it's a kind of museum story." He sighed. "But now it looks as if the story won't be in either the *Random Review* or the *Gilliland Museum Bulletin*."

Jay hung up.

He told Cindy about his conversation with Mr. Waller. "Now Mr. Pruitt is missing, too," Jay said, frowning.

"I'm more worried about Dexter," said Cindy.

"Remember, Dexter said that he thought there was something suspicious about that old farmhouse?"

Cindy nodded.

"Well, he wanted to go back and look around some time when we were with him. Maybe he's gone out there alone."

"But why would he do that?" Cindy asked.

"Maybe he thought there was something wrong. Maybe—" Jay snapped his fingers. "Maybe he decided that the mummy's mask was somehow connected with the farmhouse."

Cindy stared at Jay. "I was thinking about what Mom said last night. About how sometimes people steal things like old ancient treasures from excavation sites and then sell them to someone else. And then that person sells them, and so on."

Jay nodded, listening.

"Well someone really could be doing that, and maybe gathering all the things together in one place. And then shipping them all out . . ."

Cindy gasped. "Crates," she whispered. "Dexter saw crates. Maybe there was a shipment of stolen things out at that farmhouse. Things from digs. Masks." She put her hand to her mouth. "Dexter thinks something's going on at that old farmhouse. I bet he's out there."

"That's where he is! Maybe he's in trouble," said Jay softly. He sprang to his feet. "Let's go!"

"But we don't know where the place is," said Cindy desperately. "Just an old farmhouse, that's all he told us."

Jay shut his eyes. "He said something else. Wait a minute." His eyes flew open.

"It's half of sixteen miles," he said excitedly. "Remember, he said it was exactly sixteen miles on his odometer from his house to the deserted farmhouse and back. That means exactly eight miles each way. I'll set the mileage gauge on my bike at zero. Let's go."

"But which direction?" asked Cindy. They stared at each other, trying to remember something more.

"He sold an ad," said Cindy slowly. "To a woman at Abe's Market. That's about eight miles from here."

"On the country road," added Jay. He jumped up. "We just have to go eight miles from Dexter's house, exactly eight. That's where we'll find the farmhouse."

"Let's hurry," urged Cindy, glancing at the kitchen clock. It was past seven o'clock. "We've got to warn him. He might start poking around out there, and someone might come. Someone might find him."

Jay started for the door. "Maybe he's already been discovered," he said. "Let's go!"

They ran to get their bikes.

"Here," said Jay, reaching into the saddlebag under his seat. "We'll need these reflecting armbands. It will be dark before we get back."

Cindy glanced anxiously at the sky. "Or before

we get there," she said. "What about flashlights? Mine's here in my saddlebag."

"So's mine," said Jay.

Soon they had cycled away from the Random Street neighborhood and were heading toward the country road. By now the sun had sunk below the horizon, leaving only a few thin trails of pink and orange behind the trees.

"Maybe he won't be there after all," said Jay.

"I feel in my bones that he is," said Cindy.

"Maybe he saw the crooks. Maybe he followed them somewhere," Jay suggested.

"That's possible. But if he has gone, he'll probably have left us a clue. You know him."

"Yes, and he knows us," said Jay. "He knows if he got into any trouble we'd figure out where he was and get there to save him."

A stiff breeze had come up, and the large trees that lined the country road creaked and groaned in the darkness. Jay and Cindy pedaled for a long time in silence.

"How much farther do you think it is?" asked Cindy at last, watching the light from her small headlight bump over the pavement in front of her.

"About two miles," Jay said, looking at his mileage gauge. "We've already gone almost six miles, and we haven't reached that store Dexter told us about. After that, it's not much farther."

"There!" Cindy said a few minutes later. Up ahead was a faint glow. They could just barely make out the lettering on a sign. Abe's Market. Soon they could see the little store Dexter had described.

"Now we're close," Jay said, lowering his voice. "Keep an eye out for the driveway to the farm. It should be exactly eight miles from where we started." He kept checking his odometer while Cindy peered through the darkness.

"He said on the left," Jay reminded Cindy.

Cindy braked. "Jay," she said in a whisper, pointing. Far off, on a side road to the left, was the outline of a house. A faint light shone, somewhere in the back.

"Now to find out what's happening," said Jay soberly.

"Maybe Dexter is just having a snack with a couple who had decided to buy the farmhouse," suggested Cindy.

Jay looked at her.

"Maybe," she added.

"You're not afraid, are you?" Jay asked, staring down the long driveway to the flickering lights in the house. "Because I am."

"A little," Cindy said. "We'd better be careful in case there's no nice couple visiting with Dexter. Let's turn off our headlights and walk the bikes. That way no one will see us."

"Good idea," Jay said, getting off his bike and turning off the light. They slowly walked their bikes over the rutted, overgrown driveway.

"I can't see a thing," Cindy whispered, trying to widen her eyes in the dark.

"Me, neither," Jay whispered back. "Let's concentrate on the light. It's behind the house."

"Right," Cindy said, nearly stumbling over a clump of weeds. Her hands felt damp on her handlebars. She knew she was frightened.

They were very close to the house now, and they smelled the mustiness that Dexter had smelled earlier. Then they heard voices.

Was Dexter's voice among them? It was impossible to tell, the sounds were too muffled.

Jay touched Cindy's arm and motioned for her to follow him. She nodded, then realized that it was too dark for Jay to see her. She followed him as he very slowly crept around to the left of the house.

There were bushes everywhere, and Jay walked, unseeing, into a scraggly clump of them. Cindy bumped into him and gasped. They both lost their balance and tumbled with their bikes into the shrubbery.

Their eyes wide in the dark, Cindy and Jay froze, branches poking and pricking them. Had anyone heard the crash? They strained to hear the voices inside, but all was silent. Was someone coming out to investigate?

Cindy's throat felt tight. What would happen if they were discovered? Suddenly the voices started again. No one was coming outside. She let her breath out slowly and evenly.

Very quietly and very carefully, Jay and Cindy tried to untangle themselves from the bushes and their bikes. As Jay pulled aside a branch, his hand touched rubber and metal. He closed his fingers around whatever it was, his heart pounding. Another bike! Not an old rusty bike that might have been lost for years, but a smooth new bike. Was it Dexter's?

Jay leaned close to Cindy and whispered, "I think I've just found Dexter's bike."

Cindy stiffened and nodded. By now they were standing up, rubbing their scratched arms. They both looked carefully at the bike. It was Dexter's, all right.

"Let's leave our bikes with Dexter's," suggested Jay, still whispering in Cindy's ear. "No one will find them here."

Cindy nodded again. Now what do we do? she wondered.

It seemed as if Jay heard her thought. "Now let's try to get a look inside," Jay said. "We have to see if Dexter's in there."

The two sneaked as quietly as they possibly could past the bushes toward the back of the house where the lights were.

Suddenly Cindy pulled Jay's sleeve. She pointed to Lon's Lawn Service truck.

"Hank," said Jay in a whisper. "Do you think he's here?"

Their eyes searched the darkness. There was

another vehicle, too. A new van—the one Dexter had told them about yesterday.

There were only two windows and one door along the back wall of the house. The steps leading to the door were rotted and slanted. One of the windows belonged to what looked like an attached shed.

Cindy nudged Jay in the dim light and gestured to him that she was going to try to look through the lighted window.

"I'm coming with you," he whispered softly.

They crept silently over the deep grass and reached the window. It was just above their heads. Cindy noticed that the glass was filthy, smudged with soot and dirt. Good, she thought with relief. No one would be able to see her even if he was staring right at her. She stood on her tiptoes and locked her knees. Now she could hear voices and even pick out an occasional word. But she didn't hear Dexter.

Slowly, carefully, Cindy scraped a tiny hole with her thumbnail and put her eye to it. It was like peering through a microscope.

She could see into a bare room lit by the

flickering light of a Coleman lantern. Crates were stacked against the wall. A cellar door in the floor was propped open. There were two people in the room, a man and a woman.

The woman was talking in a scratchy, rough voice. She was a big person, but not fat, Cindy thought. The woman looked strong, and she had thick wrists and heavy arms. Her coarse, dark hair was cropped close to her large head, and the stub of a cigarette dangled loosely from the side of her wide mouth.

As Cindy watched, the woman leaned over the cellar door.

"Come on, we haven't got all night," she said.

Cindy felt panicky. Where was Dexter?

The woman spoke again. "Anson, have you got the inventory list?"

The man, too, was big and had dark, coarse hair. He was smoking a pipe. Cindy remembered that Dexter had mentioned the smell of pipe tobacco. "Right here," the man said gruffly. "We'll check everything off before we go." He spoke with an accent of some kind.

Suddenly Cindy stiffened. Hank was coming up from the cellar, and he was pulling a big box up onto the floor.

"Well, it's about time," the woman said coldly. Hank stood silent. The woman shoved him away and glanced into the box. She made notes on her clipboard. "How many more?" she asked Hank.

"Just two," Hank said. Cindy could see that Hank was sweating.

"Well, then, get moving!" the woman said. "Get the van loaded!"

Cindy dropped down to the ground. "Hank's coming outside!" she whispered to Jay. "We've got to hide." Jay grabbed Cindy's hand, and they fought their way into a clump of bushes. Just as they crouched down, Hank lurched out of the house with the box. The wooden steps creaked wildly.

Cindy held her breath. The branches of the bushes were still moving. What if Hank noticed and came over to investigate? Cindy and Jay heard Hank grunt and shove the box into the van. Then the steps creaked again. Cindy let out her breath. They hadn't been caught.

"Did you see Dex?" Jay whispered. Cindy shook her head. She told Jay what she had seen and heard.

"Maybe Dexter is hiding outside here somewhere," she added, trying to peer through the thick undergrowth.

"He would have signaled to us," Jay said. "He's got to be inside." He stood up quietly. "Hank will keep going in and out to load the van. We can't stay here."

"We've got to get inside," Cindy said.

Jay nodded in the dark and helped Cindy to her feet. The dull light shining from the back door made the drops of dew on the shrubbery glitter. Then Jay's eyes caught a different sparkle, a different glint of light. Something was shining right in front of him, hanging on a branch. He reached for the object, his eyes wide.

Cindy felt Jay move and inched closer. Then she saw what he was looking at.

Dexter's glasses, caught on a branch, swayed in front of the two Spotlighters.

Cindy clapped her hand to her mouth and stared at the dew-covered glasses. Jay lifted them from the branch and put them carefully in his pocket.

Dexter *was* in danger. They had to find him. Now!

8 • A Strange Cough

WHERE WAS DEXTER? Jay felt frightened. He shook himself sternly. It was up to him and Cindy to find Dexter and help him.

Jay stared at the rotted porch steps leading to the door. No, he thought, he couldn't go in that way. He'd be caught before he stepped on the porch. The boards would either squeak loudly, or worse, crash to the ground under his weight. He had to think of something else. His eyes moved to the dark window of the shed-like structure attached to the house. Maybe he could get the window open and climb through. He whispered his plans to

Cindy and she nodded. "I'll be right behind you," she said.

"All right," Jay said. "But once we're inside we can't say a word. Not even whisper. We'll use sign language."

They crept slowly along the side of the house until they came to the dark window in the shed. Jay reached up and felt for the frame of the dirty window. He got a grip and pushed slowly. Nothing. The window didn't budge. Had it been painted shut years before? Jay refused to give up. He tried again and, to his amazement, felt the window move. It made a slight scraping sound, and Jay stopped, listening for a different sound from within the house. He could hear the voices speaking as calmly as he had before. Good. He raised the window all the way.

He felt Cindy tug at his sleeve. Her hands clasped together, she was ready to give him a boost.

Jay's heart pounded, but he grasped the ledge of the window and placed his foot on Cindy's hands. In a moment he was inside the small, dark room. As quietly as he could, he reached out and helped pull Cindy up.

They stood motionless, listening to the low voices coming from the next room.

Jay saw a thin strip of light across the room, on the floor, and realized with relief that there was a door leading to the rest of the house. Now they had to figure out how to get into the other rooms. They had to find Dexter.

Cindy stood close to Jay, her hands clenched into fists. Dexter had to be somewhere in this house. What if he'd been caught? If Hank and those people had hurt him any way . . . She closed her eyes and tried to think clearly. Had Dexter stumbled onto something big? Something dangerous?

Jay nudged Cindy with his elbow and gestured to her that he was going to the door. He started forward, but in the dark he banged his knee against a sharp corner. He tensed, motionless. Too late. He'd been heard. The voices stopped. The floor creaked with the sound of footsteps.

"No, it's nothing," said the man, finally. "Our nerves are on edge. Let's get out of here. I never want to see this place again."

"You'll never have to," said the woman. "The

old place goes on sale next week. I've already made arrangements."

"Let's go," urged the man.

The man and woman were leaving! Cindy breathed a sigh of relief.

Jay reached down to rub his leg and felt the box he had bumped into. It was a long crate of some kind, made of wooden slats. There was a lid on it, removable. He shifted the lid. Yes, it was loose. Was this one of the crates Dexter had seen—one of the crates the crooks used for packing their stolen goods?

He reached for Cindy and directed her hands to the crate. She nodded. He knew that she recognized it as one of the crates Dexter had described.

They heard Hank going out of the house again.

Jay and Cindy stood side by side next to the crate. It was warm in the musty room, even with the window open. The palms of Cindy's hands were damp—from the heat and from worry about Dexter. How were they ever going to get into the next rooms and find him?

Suddenly there was a muffled noise close to

them. Had the man and woman in the next room been listening against the door? Were they going to burst into the little room and discover Jay and Cindy? No—the voices droned on as before.

Then what had they heard? It had sounded like a cough, Cindy decided. She wondered if Hank had crept over to the window and was peering in at Jay and her. But no—she could hear Hank's voice in the other room. She heard him say that everything was nearly ready to go. So it wasn't Hank who had coughed.

Cindy took a deep breath and gently sat down on the lid of the crate.

Suddenly she reached out for Jay's arm, digging in her fingernails.

Someone was in the crate.

Jay instantly turned to her and leaned close. Cindy grabbed Jay's hands and put them on the lid of the crate. Together they lifted the lid and placed it on the floor.

Jay reached his hand into the crate and felt a face.

His heart lurched, and he instinctively withdrew his hand, nearly falling backward. He caught himself, his heart pounding. He had felt a face, all right. He could still feel the dampness on his hand—dampness from a face drenched in sweat.

Could the person in the crate be Dexter?

Now Jay could hear breathing coming in shallow gasps. It had to be Dexter. Jay reached down again, and felt a sweat shirt and rough rope . . . Dexter?

It was Dexter.

Jay felt around in his pocket for his knife and hurriedly, in the dark, cut Dexter's ropes.

Dexter was weak. Jay and Cindy carefully

helped him out of the crate and rubbed his arms and legs where the rope had dug in. They stood listening. Hank was in the next room with the man and woman. The Spotlighters had to get away before he went outside again.

Silently, Jay and Cindy helped Dexter over to the window. Jay was the first to climb out. Cindy helped Dexter over the ledge, and then she followed.

They moved quickly, Jay and Cindy on each side of Dexter, supporting him. Soon they were yards away, in the deep, waving grass behind the house.

"Let's lie down," Jay whispered, keeping his eye on the house. He was sure no one could hear their voices from here. Dexter and Cindy lay down, their chins resting on their fists.

"For a minute there, I thought I'd never see you two again," Dexter said, trying to joke.

"You had us scared to death," Cindy said. "We found your bike, and we found your glasses."

"Here they are," said Jay, producing them from his pocket.

Gratefully, Dexter put his glasses on. "You sat on me," Dexter said, his voice filled with a giddiness

Cindy knew was relief. She felt relieved, too, and couldn't help giggling. The three Spotlighters lay in the grass staring at the old house. They saw Hank lug another crate from inside the house to the van.

"Tell us what happened, Dex," Jay urged.

Dexter told Jay and Cindy how he had been captured and what Hank had told him. "I couldn't make any noise inside the crate," he explained. "I didn't know what would happen if those two crooks found out I was there. But I just couldn't hold my cough in anymore. When you bumped into the crate, I didn't know if you were Hank or one of the other two. I just had to keep quiet."

"Thank heaven you coughed," Cindy said.

The three detectives were quiet again. The long grass around them rustled in the wind. They were trying to think what to do next.

"Let's find our bikes and get out of here," said Cindy.

Jay started to his feet. Then he knelt down and whispered, "Those crooks will get away for good with all the treasures they've stolen."

Jay wound a long blade of grass around his finger. "We have to get the police. But we can't all go. Two of us should stay and keep an eye on them, try to keep them here somehow." He unwound the grass and sat up. "I'll go for help. I know there are some houses around somewhere. I can find a phone. And I'll be back as soon as I can with the police."

Dexter sat up. He rubbed his wrists. "They're planning to leave tonight. Right away. All they have to do is load up the van with those crates of stolen goods, and they'll vanish. For good."

"Maybe they won't be able to leave," Cindy said.

Jay and Dexter stared at her.

"What if we make sure their trucks won't start?" she said slowly. "There must be dozens of ways to do that."

Jay nodded eagerly. "That's perfect, Cindy. It's a perfect way to keep them here. And they wouldn't leave their van, filled with all that treasure. They'd have to stay—until the police arrive."

"We'll take care of the truck and van," Dexter said. "You go for the police, Jay."

The Spotlighters stood up. A gust of wind swept over the grass, making a chorus of animal-like noises.

"I think it's better if I go on foot," Jay said, whispering again. "I'll go over the fields. I'd make too much noise getting my bike out of the bushes. And I'd probably get stuck in the long grass and ruts."

Dexter and Cindy nodded, glancing across the dark, hilly expanse of country that Jay would have to cross.

Dexter felt in his pocket. "I didn't bring my knife, Jay. Can I use yours? For the tires."

Jay handed him his knife and quickly disappeared in the dark of the countryside.

Cindy and Dexter saw that Hank was nowhere in sight. They headed for the truck and the van, crouching low and not speaking. Dexter worked quickly, slashing the tough rubber of the tires while Cindy kept her eyes on the house. By the time Dexter was finished, the vehicles had sunk perceptibly closer to the ground. The crooks would never get away now.

Then Cindy and Dexter crawled silently, in single file, back through the long grass to their hiding place. Now all they had to do was wait for Jay. And the police.

9 · *Journey in the Night*

JAY RAN STEADILY across the dark field. He remembered seeing a light in a house when he and Cindy were on their bikes. That house couldn't be too far. Without his flashlight, Jay stumbled twice in the dark. But he didn't dare use the light until he had run farther.

When he thought he had put enough distance between himself and the old farmhouse, he looked back over his shoulder. The lights from the farmhouse barely shone. Now he could safely use his flashlight without being seen. He flicked it on and began to run again, his feet following the small circle of light.

And suddenly he saw it, a light flickering beyond a small cluster of trees. A house. With a telephone. Jay hurried through the trees.

The house was just at the edge of a small woods. He saw the glow from a porch light and another light, faint, shining from somewhere within the house.

In his haste, Jay slipped on the long, dewy grass near the front porch. He picked himself up and hurried up the steps, shutting off his flashlight. There was no doorbell, so he pounded on the door. He tried to think what he would say on the telephone to the police. He leaned against the door, waiting for it to be opened.

No one answered. Jay banged again, frustrated. He felt the blood pounding in his head and tried to stay calm. Dexter and Cindy were counting on him to come through. He had to get to the phone inside.

Jay peered through the window in the door. He saw a neat, clean living room, but no people.

Wasn't anyone home? He was so close to a telephone—he could see one on a small table next to a chair. He knocked again, loudly. Maybe the owners were at the back of the house and couldn't hear him. It was a big house. They could be in the basement, even.

Jay dashed down the steps and headed toward the back. It was dark, and he flicked on his flashlight again. The circle of light seemed dimmer than before. Oh, no, were the batteries going dead? He turned the flashlight off. He reached the back porch and pounded on the door, peering in the window. An empty, clean kitchen was all he saw.

Jay didn't want to believe what he knew was true. No one was home. He leaned against the porch railing, feeling helpless. He was so close, so very close.

He had to get to the phone inside, he couldn't give up. Was there a chance that someone had left the door unlocked? Jay reached for the doorknob and turned it. No, the door was locked. A window, then?

To his right was a low window, low enough, he hoped, to climb through. As he felt around the edges of the frame, he saw movement inside. A dark shape drew close to the window. Jay stopped. If someone was inside, why hadn't that person

answered the door? Jay peered in. There it was again, a dark shadow, moving silently toward him.

And suddenly Jay's knees trembled. He was staring into the very dark, very large eyes of a Doberman.

The dog's lips were pulled back over its long pointed teeth, and saliva was gathering at the edge of its mouth. Jay could hear a low, menacing growl coming from the dog's throat.

Jay jumped back, almost falling. He wouldn't stand a chance against a guard dog like that. He left the back of the house and, heart still pounding, hurried to the front yard.

He would have to find another house, another telephone. He looked around at the swaying trees and open, empty fields. This was farm country. There were other farmers and other houses. There had to be.

He tested his flashlight and saw with dismay that his batteries were fading. He would have to save the light for an emergency. As if this wasn't an emergency!

The night was empty, quiet, and dark. Jay saw no other lights. He felt like shouting in frustration at the house behind him.

Suddenly he slapped his palm against his forehead. That little country store—the place Dexter had gone yesterday to get an ad. What was it called? Abe's Market. Dexter had said that the woman lived there, above the store. If only he had remembered before! Then he could have taken his bike and headed down the road, instead of struggling through dark fields and woods.

Jay knew he couldn't afford the time to go back and get his bike. He'd just find the country road and the little store on foot. The road had to be beyond that field, he was sure.

It was hard going without his flashlight, but Jay kept on. He finally saw a dark band ahead. The road. He wondered how far he had gone already, how close he was to Abe's Market. Had he run a mile? More?

His eyes searched the road. Was there a chance a car would come along? There was nothing in sight. Very few people used this road at night, Jay knew.

Just as he reached the road he saw the same faint glow of light he and Cindy had seen on their way to the farmhouse. That was it! The little store. It was still a couple of hundred yards away, and Jay picked up speed in the dark. He planted his feet carefully, trying not to stumble.

Suddenly he slipped, and his foot twisted. With a cry of pain he fell to the gravel at the side of the road.

Slowly Jay stood up, furious with himself for hurting his ankle. He rubbed it, and he could tell it wasn't broken. He knew that much from his first-aid class at school. The ankle did hurt, though—he might have a bad sprain. But there was nothing he could do about it right now. He forced himself to get up and hobbled onto the dark pavement of the road.

He walked slowly, limping, toward the glow of light from the little store. He used his fading flashlight now, not wanting to risk another stumble. Every minute counted for Dexter and Cindy.

As he neared the store, Jay saw with immense relief the figure of a woman moving about behind an upstairs window. He could be talking to the police within two minutes. He switched off his flashlight and leaned against the glass door of the store. There was a small button next to the door. Jay pushed it and heard a loud ringing.

He waited, listening for the sound of footsteps. Peering in through the glass door, he saw neat shelves stretching to the back of the store. A small light bulb hung from the ceiling. When nobody appeared, Jay rang the bell again, and again he peered in. There was the woman, still busily moving around. Couldn't she hear the bell? Frustrated, Jay jabbed the button again. Then he remembered with a hopeless, sinking feeling that Dexter had said the woman didn't hear very well. Deaf, almost.

He stood, his weight on his good ankle, feeling alone and helpless. "Oh, no," he groaned aloud.

Then he hammered his fists against the door. He would *make* her hear him.

10 • Where Is Jay?

WHILE JAY WAS at Abe's Market, Cindy and Dexter hid in the long grass, keeping their eyes on the old farmhouse. So much time had passed already. Where was Jay?

Hank, Anson, and the woman would be getting ready to leave soon.

"They're going to be very, very surprised. And very, very mad," whispered Dexter. "They'll be all ready to go, everything loaded up—and whammo! They won't be able to drive the truck away." He grinned.

It seemed funny to Cindy, too, and she stifled a giggle. "And just as they're wondering what has happened, the police will come," she said.

"We've really done it right this time," Dexter said, feeling proud. "Well, you and Jay have. If it hadn't been for you two, I'd still be tied up in that stuffy old crate."

Dexter was silent, thinking about the endless time he had been tied up. Then he went on in a whisper. "We know enough for the police to arrest Hank and the other two. Even if we don't know who they are or where they're going, the treasures in those crates are enough evidence."

Crickets were chirping around Dexter and Cindy, and the long grass almost seemed to whistle softly in the wind. Suddenly Dexter grabbed Cindy's arm, pressing it hard. She sucked in her breath. Hank and the woman and man were coming out of the house. The two Spotlighters could hear their voices and the loud, complaining groans of the rotten steps.

"You get the light," the woman said. Her voice sounded harsh and angry. Cindy and Dexter could see that she carried a clipboard in her hand.

"How we could be missing that valuable mask is beyond me," she said.

The mask, Cindy thought. The mask Jay had found, the mask Hank had hidden in Mr. Priutt's yard.

The man spoke next. "Relax. We've got enough as it is, enough to see us to Europe and beyond."

"But that mask would have brought us even more money," the woman said bitterly. "Where could it be?"

Hank was silent. He stood still, his beefy arms at his sides.

"I said to get the light," the woman said again, her voice rising shrilly. She pointed at Hank, who quickly retreated into the house. In a moment the farmhouse was plunged into darkness. Dexter and Cindy could see nothing now, but they heard the steps creak again. Hank had come back out of the house.

"Where's the torch?" the man, Anson, asked. "How can you expect to see in this awful dark? For being such a well-organized group, we certainly seem to have our failings, don't we, dear?"

The two Spotlighters heard the woman hiss loudly. "Hank, get the torch for Anson. The sooner we get out of here, the better."

In a few minutes Hank had switched on a flashlight.

"Now," the woman said loudly, in charge again, "let's get rolling. Hank, you take your truck. We'll follow in my van. Then it's all over."

Hank's flashlight produced a bright, strong beam in front of the three of them. They walked with purpose to their trucks.

"This is it," Dexter whispered to Cindy. Cindy looked at the road beyond the field. Where was Jay? Where were the police? They had to get here soon.

Suddenly there was an explosion of angry voices, and Cindy and Dexter crouched lower. They heard someone hit a fist against metal and peered through the grass to see the woman pounding her van. "All the tires slashed! How can we get out of here now?"

Dexter and Cindy watched the beam of light from Hank's flashlight. It played on the tires, around the ground, and near the house. Their plan had worked. The trucks couldn't leave now. Dexter and Cindy silently shook hands and grinned in the dark.

"We're going to get to the bottom of this," the woman said viciously. Dexter and Cindy saw her grab the flashlight from Hank. "Someone's been here in the last hour. He's probably here now."

Hank and Anson were silent. The woman moved away from them. She started slowly around the house, flashing her light in all directions.

Cindy swallowed. She hadn't expected anybody would have time to look for the tire slashers. She thought the police would have come long before now. But there the woman was, circling the house, determined to find a clue.

"Our bikes," Cindy whispered desperately to Dexter. "What if she finds them?"

"They're in the bushes. She'll never find them. Besides," he added, "Jay will be here with the police any minute."

He and Cindy lay in the grass, their hearts pounding. They could see the light bouncing in front of the house, then to the side. Suddenly there was a shout. Cindy clutched a handful of grass.

The woman had found the bikes.

Cindy and Jay heard Hank and Anson running toward the light. "Just lie still. They won't find us," said Dexter.

The woman stalked to the back of the house. The two men followed. "Turn the lantern on," the woman said. "We'll want all the light we can get to find them. They must be here somewhere. They wouldn't get far without those bikes."

"Come on, Jay," Cindy urged, trying again to see something on the road. But there were no headlights, no police cars coming to rescue them.

"Get my spotlight from the van," the woman ordered. "If anyone's around here, we'll find out." Dexter and Cindy saw Hank go to the woman's van and open a door. In a moment he returned with a large, circular object.

"Turn it on," the woman ordered Hank. The yard was filled with blinding light, and Cindy and Dexter instinctively ducked, their chins thrust on the cold, damp grass. They felt exposed and obvious in their hiding place. Each blade of grass ahead of them looked clear and vivid, as though in sunlight. Could they stay hidden? Would the grass

be enough to keep them from view? Cindy wanted to reach over and hold onto Dexter's arm, but she didn't dare move.

The bright light wavered, painfully bright, over the yard, and suddenly there was a shout from the woman. "There in the grass!" Cindy's eyes closed. They had been seen, after all. She didn't know whether to lie as quietly as she could or jump up with Dexter and make a run for it. Where was Jay—where *was* he?

The two Spotlighters felt the earth in front of them shake with heavy footsteps. Dexter grabbed Cindy's arm and pulled her up with him. He thrust Cindy behind him and stood facing the woman and the men.

Hank stopped dead in his tracks, dropping the bright light. He looked as though he had seen a ghost. And no wonder, Dexter thought. Hank still thought Dexter was tied up in that stuffy old crate.

"You clumsy oaf," the woman said angrily to Hank, bending to pick up the spotlight. She shone it on Dexter and Cindy, full in their faces. "So you're the mean little devils who slashed my tires!" Her voice was menacing, deep, and angry. "Bring them with me," she said to Hank and Anson. She turned on her heel, swinging the light in front of her.

Rough, big hands closed over Dexter's and Cindy's arms, and the two of them were yanked through the tall grass.

Cindy glanced at Dexter. His eyes stared straight ahead. His mouth was straight. Why couldn't she be that brave? She thought she was going to scream. Jay! she yelled inside her head. Where are you?

They were dragged back to the house, their arms hurting from the men's strong hands. The woman waited there, her thick arms folded. The spotlight rested by her feet.

"Where's the other one?" she demanded angrily. "There were three bikes. Where's the other one?" Her eyes, dark and large, now squinted into slits.

Cindy knew she and Dexter mustn't tell where Jay was. If the crooks suspected that the police were coming, they'd run. And what would they do with her and Dexter?

Dexter spoke. Cindy was amazed at how calm

and natural his voice sounded. "He was just here a few minutes ago," he said. "I don't know where he is. He said he wanted to look around a little, that's all. But he should be somewhere nearby, that's for sure."

The woman squinted at him.

"It's true," Cindy said suddenly, hoping she sounded convincing. "We were just talking in the grass, the three of us, ten minutes ago. And then he decided to scout around. We were just going to run away."

The woman looked from Dexter to Cindy and back again. Hank and Anson hung in the background, not speaking.

"Then your little friend will be back in a minute or two, I trust," she said.

"Yes, he will," Cindy answered. Yes, he will, she said to herself. With the police.

"Then we'll wait for him. In the basement," the woman said, her eyes glinting now. "He'll come looking for you. Hank," she said, turning, "get the rope from the van. And bring it downstairs." Hank went silently to the van, and Anson shoved Dexter and Cindy in front of him.

"As soon as we take care of these vandals, we'll get another truck," she said, speaking to herself out loud. "We'll still get away. We'll still get away."

Dexter and Cindy were pushed up the stairs behind the woman. She led the way to the cellar door.

"Get down in there," she commanded roughly to Dexter and Cindy, shoving them. "Anson, make sure you tie them up tight, understand?"

"My pleasure," Anson said.

Cindy swallowed. Anson grabbed her elbow and nearly dragged her down the steep ladder that led to the basement. Dexter was right behind her. The basement was cold and damp and pitch-black.

"Throw me down a flashlight!" Anson called.

Suddenly Dexter and Cindy heard shouting. The house above them creaked and groaned with the running of feet.

"What the—?" Anson started to shout.

"It's the police!" the woman screamed.

Anson headed up the steep ladder, his mind obviously bent on escape. Dexter and Cindy crowded behind him. They were safe now. Jay had come at last!

In a moment they were outside. The backyard was a scene of total confusion, with uniformed policemen chasing the fleeing thieves. Spotlights shone from the squad cars. Dexter and Cindy searched the yard for Jay. At last they saw him limping toward them. They raced over to him, and the detectives hugged each other.

"I thought I'd never get back here," Jay said, out of breath. "The first house I came to was empty. There was a guard dog. And then I remembered the store you went to, Dex. It took that lady forever to hear me, but finally she did. And I finally talked to the police. They said they had just received a phone call from Mr. Pruitt. Mr. Pruitt told the police that the mask was obviously a stolen one and very valuable. I guess he'd told his friends not to come after all, because he had to take the mask into Chicago, to a specialist to have it evaluated."

Jay paused to take a breath. "So when I called the police and told them what I knew and what was happening, they put everything together. They came to the store and picked me up there."

"You're limping," Cindy said with concern. "What happened?"

Jay explained. "But to tell the truth," he said, "I feel so great now I hardly notice my ankle."

"What an article we'll have for the next issue of the *Random Review,*" Dexter said proudly.

"And this time we'll have our names in it, right, Cindy?" Jay asked with a grin.

"In headlines," Cindy agreed.

The three Spotlighters slung their arms around each other and walked toward the police cars.

About the authors Florence Parry Heide and Roxanne Heide have no trouble thinking of exciting adventures for the Spotlight Club detectives. Often this mother-daughter team meet at a family lakeside cottage in Wisconsin, spend several days with their typewriters, and emerge with the plot for a story. More conferences, phone calls, letters, and perhaps another meeting, and a new mystery is ready.

Florence Heide brings versatility and enthusiasm to all she does. She's written lyrics for songs, picture books (including the popular THE SHRINKING OF TREEHORN), short novels for teen readers, and stories for reading programs, as well as the Spotlight Club mystery series. Roxanne Heide has produced textbook material and collaborated on many mysteries in the Spotlight Club series, as well as on the Brillstone mysteries, another series published by Albert Whitman.

About the illustrator Seymour Fleishman is a Chicago artist who has worked in book illustration, advertising, and design. He has illustrated many books for children, including the Spotlight Club series. Mr. Fleishman has also written and illustrated PRINTCRAFTS, a book that presents ways children can print their own stationery, announcements, and newspapers.